ALPHABOO!

A
HIDDEN LETTER
ABC BOOK

Can you find all the letters
Hidden in this book?
It's fun and not that hard to do.
Just use your eyes and look!

Grosset & Dunlap

ALPHABOO!

A
HIDDEN LETTER
ABC BOOK

By Carol Thompson

Illustrated by Margaret A. Hartelius

Magic Mirror

ON THE WAY OUT

DOWN AND OUT

BIG SURPRISE

FAR OUT

NO WAY OUT

Grosset & Dunlap, Publishers

Text copyright © 1994 by Carol Thompson. Illustrations copyright © 1994 by Margaret A. Hartelius. All rights reserved. Published by Grosset & Dunlap, a division of Penguin Putnam Books for Young Readers, New York. GROSSET & DUNLAP is a trademark of Grosset & Dunlap, Inc. Published simultaneously in Canada. Printed in the U.S.A. Library of Congress Catalog Card Number: 93-26925
ISBN 0-448-40213-0   E F G H I J

A a

An awesome army of arms
Is stirring the alphabet stew.
But there's one letter missing,
And they need some help from you!

Find 6 **A**'s
Find 3 **a**'s

What things in the picture begin with A?

B b

Find 4 **B**'s
Find 3 **b**'s

Bat, baby, bottle,
Blanket, and ball—
Can you find the letter
That begins them all?

What things in the picture begin with B?

C c

Find 2 **C**'s

Find 4 **C**'s

General Store

Fat-Free

Yummies

RED HOTS

Spider Cider

Gummy Legs 5¢ a pair

PICKLES 2 NICKELS

All the creepy crawlies
Think this store is just dandy.
Help them find some letters now.
They're hidden in the candy.

What things in the picture begin with C?

Find 3 **D**'s
Find 4 **d**'s

Dragon's on the doorstep
In a brand-new dress.
What's her favorite letter?
Well, just take a guess!

What things in the picture begin with D?

E e

STARSHIP

SHOOTING STAR

Find 3 **E**'s
Find 6 **e**'s

BLACK HOLE

ORBIT ORANGE

GALAXY GREEN

GRAVITY GRAY

Extraterrestrials at their easels
Think painting's extra-fun.
Can you find some hidden letters?
There's paint on every one!

What things in the picture begin with E?

Find 5 **F**'s

Find 6 **f**'s

Fang's fantastic fireworks
Fly so far and fast and high,
That they light up all the letters
Hiding in the midnight sky.

What things in the picture begin with F?

G g

Find 5 **G**'s
Find 4 **g**'s

Da Bones

Today - Ghosts vs Da Bones

BONES

A gang of ghosts glides toward the goal—
No one can stop this shot.
The fans all keep on cheering;
Those ghosts are really hot!

What things in the picture begin with G?

H h

Find 2 **H**'s
Find 2 **h**'s

HAIR-RAISING CLUB
MONSTERS ONLY !!!!

Hairdo hangs the hammock up;
Hairdon't hauls supplies.
Hunt for secret clubhouse letters
If you have sharp eyes!

What things in the picture begin with H?

Ii

Cooler Droolers

13¢

Rent-A-Board

Find 3 **I**'s
Find 5 **i**'s

SKATEBOARDING!
ICE-SKATING!
SWIMMING!

KEEP OFF

"I say! It is I,
The Invisible Man!
I inch past hidden letters—
Look and find them if you can."

What things in the picture begin with I?

J j

Find 4 **J**'s
Find 2 **j**'s

WATCH OUT for the PUMPKIN EATER!

PUMPKIN PATCH PAL

TRICK or TREAT

TRICK OR TREAT

TRICK or TREAT

TRICK or TREAT

Slurp

Jill and Jack-O'-Lantern
Think that trick-or-treating's neat.
Do you see the letters jumping
On their jumbo bags of treats?

What things in the picture begin with J?

K k

Find 4 **K**'s
Find 5 **k**'s

SCAREPORT

DEPARTURES

SNACKS

ARRIVALS

DOWN

BAGGAGE

CHECK-IN

Oh, no! Oh, dear! Kisser's here!
A simple "Hi!" won't do.
Better find the hidden letters
Or you might get kiss-kissed, too!

What things in the picture begin with K?

L l

Little leeches in the lunchroom
Look for letters they can chew.
Give a seat to little leeches
Or they'll sit on top of you!

Find 3 **L**'s
Find 2 **I**'s

Let's GO LEECHES!

Leech Lunch Menu
Liverwurst Soup
Leftover Liver Loaf
Liver'n' Lumps
Leeches 'n' Cream
Lemon Slime Pie

Leech Friday
we serve
Blood Pudding

suckers 10¢

FALL FOODS

SALAD BAR

Liver Sticks + Lumps

What things in the picture begin with L?

M m

Find 4 **M**'s
Find 3 **m**'s

monster's market

BAKERY

REALLY BIG BOXES

nite time

FLAKES

crummies

Monster Mix

SLURPS

Ripe or Rotten

Old Stuff

MONSTER MUFFINS

Wrapping Extra

Mummy's at the market
And she checks her shopping list.
Milk and muffins, macaroni—
Is there something that she's missed?

What things in the picture begin with M?

N n

PABLO'S PIZZA PALACE

Find 2 **N**'s
Find 3 **n**'s

Smell and Tell Pizza Contest Today!

TAKE OUT

25¢ a slice
After school
special!

F A-PIZZA

NOTES

TIMES

"I smell trouble," says Nose.
"And I'm searching for a clue."
Where are all the missing letters?
Well, Nose knows. Do you?

What things in the picture begin with N?

O o

Find 2 **O**'s
Find 3 **O**'s

Ogre's fallen overboard.
How silly can you get?
Now instead of going fishing,
Ogre's soaking wet!

What things in the picture begin with O?

P p

PURPLE PEST PET SHOW

NO POKING or PULLING

Find 6 **P**'s
Find 5 **p**'s

PIRANHA

PAT-A-PET

Purple Pests have pretty pets—
A pink poodle wins first prize.
This pet show's packed with letters
Hidden right before your eyes!

What things in the picture begin with P?

Q q

Find 2 **Q**'s
Find 3 **q**'s

ONCE UPON A SLIME

SLIMY BUBBLES

These quintuplet monsters
Don't like their bath one bit.
Can you see some letters in their tub?
Find them all—don't quit!

What things in the picture begin with Q?

R r

Find 6 **R**'s
Find 6 **r**'s

Judge
starter
stopper
timer

RAT RACE! - Every Frighty Night

PIT STOP

ZOOM BROOM

RAT-RACER

Go gator

SCAT CAT

Ratman and his ratmobile
Race 'round and 'round the ring.
Oh, no! Those letters on the road
Will slow down everything!

What things in the picture begin with R?

Find 3 **S**'s
Find 4 **S**'s

S s

SHOESTRING'S SHOES

Shine with...
Star Time Shoes

Spider shops for shoes.
He tries on every pair.
Oh, Spider, don't step
On letters everywhere!

BEACH BABIES

MONSTERS

WINGTIPS

Boots by Frank N. Stein

Skinny

FAT FOOT

What things in the picture begin with S?

T t

Find 5 **T**'s
Find 3 **t**'s

At a troll tea party, greedy guests
Can slurp from every cup.
Find all the hidden letters or
The trolls will eat them up!

What things in the picture begin with T?

U u

Find 5 **U**'s
Find 4 **u**'s

The Uglies' town is upside-down,
With flowers growing underground.
Instead of "Hi!" they say "What's down?"
And hidden letters are all around!

What things in the picture begin with U?

V v

Find 3 **V**'s

Find 2 **V**'s

VARMINT'S VIDEOS

VERY SCARY

Ghosts!

Gotcha!

Beauty and the Beast

HOWL ALONE

NEW

HOWL ALONE!

TAKE HOME POPCORN for your TAKE HOME MOVIE

POPCORN!

SCARY

MAD MOON

Terminator

WEB!

Vinnie Vampire's very fond
Of S-C-A-R-Y videos!
His favorite letter's somewhere
Right before his nose.
What things in the picture begin with V?

W w

Wrestling Spook-tacular Tonight!

Find 3 **W**'s
Find 4 **W**'s

TICKETS

25¢ A SLICE

Witches love a wrestling match
With cheers and jeers galore.
Warlock wants to win the round,
And Werewolf hits the floor.

What things in the picture begin with W?

X x

Find 6 **X**'s
Find 3 **X**'s

The X-ray Eyes check out their map.
It says "X marks the spot."
But which X? If you look around
You'll see that there are a lot!

What things in the picture begin with X?

Y y

Find 3 **Y**'s
Find 4 **y**'s

Yucky's Yogurt

15¢

Yeti's yelling "Yahoo!"
See her yellow bobsled go!
It flies across the yard
On letters hidden in the snow.

What things in the picture begin with Y?

Z z

Zombie can't stop yawning!
Guess it's time to catch some z's.
Just look carefully and you'll find them,
But remember, "QUIET PLEASE!"

Find 6 **Z**'s
Find 5 **Z**'s

ZODIAC!

CHIPS

What things in the picture begin with Z?

They're peeking out from everywhere,
Just take a look and see.
Scare up the letters hiding here,
There's one from A to Z.

Here's the whole alphabet—
Come on and take a look.
Have you found all the letters
That are hidden in this book?